THE POPCORN SHOP

by Alice Low
Illustrated by Patti Hammel

Hello Reader! — Level 3

Cartwheel
·B·O·O·K·S·™
Scholastic Inc.
New York   Toronto   London   Sydney   Auckland

Popcorn Nell
had a popcorn shop.
The popcorn there
went pop, pop, pop!

She popped the popcorn
in a pot
and sold that popcorn
piping hot.

Folks stood in line.
The line was long,
and as they stood,
they heard Nell's song:

"Popcorn popping,
pop, pop, pop!
Pour the butter
on the top.

Perfect popcorn,
come and try it.
Plenty of it,
come and buy it."

So popular
was Popcorn Nell,
she could not make
enough to sell.

And so she bought
a big machine,
the biggest one
you've ever seen.

It popped the popcorn
all day long,
and as it popped,
Nell sang this song:

"Lots of popcorn,
buy, come buy!
Popcorn pancakes,
popcorn pie.

Popcorn pickles,
popcorn stew,
Popsicles
of popcorn, too."

Now there was plenty
in the town
until that big machine
broke down.

Nell called a fix-it man
to come.
He hammered
and he tinkered some.

And as he left
he said to Nell,
"I've fixed it up.
I've fixed it well.

If you don't let it
overheat,
you'll pop more corn
than you can eat."

And sure enough,
that man was right.
The popcorn popped
both day and night.

The popcorn popped
onto the floor,
and then it popped
right out the door!

And everybody
cried, "Hooray!
Let's have
a popcorn holiday!"

That popcorn piled up
everywhere.

It filled the barber's
barber chair.

It blew through shops
with shoes and hats,

MABLE'S SHOES

and shops with puppies,
birds and cats.

They closed the market
on Main Street,

for folks had more
than they could eat.

Popcorn in
the scarecrow's clothes . . .

and popcorn in
the fire truck's hose.

Popcorn in
the postal sack,

and popcorn on
the jogging track.

Popcorn filled
the pumpkin patch
and rained down on
the tennis match.

Cars, trains and buses
couldn't go
through popcorn piled
as high as snow.

The people cried,
"Nell, make this stop.
There's too much popcorn
going POP!"

The mayor said,
"I'll call a cop
unless you make
this popping stop."

Said Popcorn Nell,
"I don't know how.
I cannot stop
this popping now."

But as she baked
her popcorn cake,
that big machine
began to shake.

It sputtered sparks,
turned red and glowed.
Cried Nell, "Watch out!
It might explode!"

It gave one loud
enormous POP!
And then at last
it blew its top.

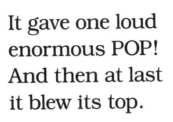

Now Popcorn Nell
is Pizza Nell,
and she makes pizza
very well.

She makes that pizza
all by hand
at Pizza Nell's
Fine Pizza Stand.

And as she works,
she sings this song:
"With pizza . . .
nothing can go wrong.

FLOU

FLOUR

No big machine
that will not stop,
and pizza won't go
POP! POP! POP!"